[Type text]

Professor Moriarty's Short Stories
Action, Satire, Eroticism, Escapism

James J. Moriarty, Jr.
12/1/2012

Synopsis: A great grandson of Professor Moriarty, a science journalist, writes semi-fiction. He demonstrates that sometimes, fiction can illustrate the truth better than formal journalism.

Ten stories detail the antics of two Federal Investigators:

MORIARTY & MEEHAN (M & M).

Professor Moriarty's great-grandson

Contents

1. A Modern Spartan Woman

    M&M   action   7

2. Spaghetti in the Panties

    M&M   humor   13

3. Body Count

    M&M   action, military   27

4. Body Count, Continued

    M&M   action, politics   34

5. Gold in Key Largo

    M&M   action, crime   44

6. Vultures in Downtown Miami

    M&M   action, crime   61

7. An Experienced Woman

    M&M   humor   86

8. A REALLY EXPERIENCED Woman

    M&M   more humor   90

9. Alcoholism and Recovery in the Keys

    M&M   psychology   99

Contents   5

10. Another Admiral Rickover Story: Character

M&M   tough men   109

11. Wikileak: BAJA, the 51st State   satire 115

12. Blanketing a Homosexual

            military history   122

13. HELP: BIG, BLACK WOMEN

            social essay   131

14. Research and Prayer

            essay + story   145

15. BAD ACTORS (Rev #5)   *screenplay = pulp fiction with muscle, posted on* www.TriggerStreet.com *160*

This page intentionally left blank...so you can use your imagination. Sir Arthur Conan Doyle did. So did Walt Disney. Now it's your turn, reader...whoever you are.

Professor James Moriarty, camped somewhere between Virginia's Blue Ridge Mountains and Key West...writing.   M

STORY #1

A Modern Spartan Woman

copyright 2012 James J. Moriarty, Jr.

Synopsis: The Spartans of Michigan State send a Marine into combat in the Vietnam War. They tell him, "Come back with your shield, not on it."

A Modern Spartan Woman

copyright 2012 James J. Moriarty, Jr.

She was a beauty…a balanced figure, girl next-door looks like Playboy—not kinky like Penthouse or sleazy like Hustler.

SPARTAN WOMAN

She was an artist who followed Freud's pleasure principle—if it made her feel good, she did it. If it gave her pain, she avoided it.

Diana, named after the Greek goddess of the hunt, was a coed at Michigan State University in the late sixties. MSU is a Big Ten university that supports the Armed Forces and treats veterans the way they deserve to be treated.

When a vet returns, the university supports them with housing, financial aid, and provides assistance for their family if they have one.

Sean Meehan, my best friend from kindergarten days, just received his orders to head to Vietnam. He was a freshly minted Second

Lieutenant, the type of officer that has a short life span in combat—they lead the troops.

He called me from Quantico, Virginia when he got his orders. Next, he called from Niagara Falls, New York. I am sure he was saying goodbye to a former girlfriend who had rejected him...not a good way to head to combat.

"Jim, I'm headed out. Take care of me," he added quarters on a pay phone—remember they used cash in the 20th century.

I gave him the house address in East Lansing, Michigan where a group of graduate/medical students lived.

The house was located two blocks from where Jim Cash later wrote <u>TOP GUN</u> (1986). He used the early Internet to communicate with a writing partner in Hollywood.

MSU is a sophisticated computer based university. We don't just play championship athletics.

Seven hours later, Sean was at the front door—a ten hour drive from Niagara Falls by any normal driving pace.

Sean's attitude was: "Dangerous? What are they going to do to me? I'm heading to a combat zone."

A full moon had set by 10:00 p.m. I handed him a good cigar and a glass of Jameson Irish whiskey. I told him to walk on down the hall to the bedroom from where light was coming. The rest of the house was dark.

The naked Spartan beauty was waiting under the lily white linen sheets [cf., Dominatrix as young woman, in the screenplay BAD ACTORS (Rev #5) www.TriggerStreet.com] .

She smiled at the handsome, fit Marine in his physical prime—fresh out of Quantico training.

She fucked and sucked him all night. She even taught him tricks which the Marine sergeants at OCS (Officers Candidate School) had baited him.

The next day, the modern Spartan woman thumped him out of bed. She smiled, and said, "Thanks, marine, I needed that. Now come back with your shield, not on it."

FADE OUT.

Story #2

Spaghetti in the Panties

copyright 2012 James J. Moriarty, Jr.

Lt. Meehan requests a "spaghetti throwing party" where the women only wear T shirts and panties. Meehan is headed to Vietnam as a forward observer, a high risk assignment.

Dr. Mendershausen provides the erotic details while he slips a plate of spaghetti into the Spartan beauty's silk panties. Pure grain alcohol is planted in the punch. The ongoing Moriarty & Meehan (M&M) short stories series continues. Action & Humor.

SPAGHETTI

DOMINATRIX [BAD ACTORS (Rev #5) www.TriggerStreet.com] liked to party.

As a young woman at Michigan State, she used to go on ski vacations at Walloon Lake, Michigan--from where Ernest Hemingway wrote his Nick Adams stories.

As I wrote in "A Modern Spartan Woman, (www.TriggerStreet.com)" Sean Meehan, my boyhood friend, was headed to Vietnam as a Second Lieutenant. He was a forward observer. He requested, no, he demanded, a final sendoff that would require "spaghetti throwing T shirts and nothing else."

We loaded an old school bus that belonged to a rock 'n roll band--Bill Sloane and his crew. Bill had a lengthy flaccid penis which he slung around in a circle to impress the girls. Sloane and the "pen wheel" is another story that can only be told on request.

20 party animals stepped forward. At MSU we not only know how to fight and win athletic championships, we know how to party!

Paul Weisbord provided a AAA card that proved useful when the bus needed a jump start in the 30 degree Michigan winter. Spartans work together.

Weisbord was a university rat, if there ever was one--he lived in the empty offices of Baker Hall adjacent to the Psychology Research Lab. He shaved at night in the men's room when no one was there. He showered in the athletic facilities and got A's in the graduate courses he took.

Paul was recruited as a National Merit Semi-finalist--Michigan State recruits intelligence the way it recruits superior athletic talent.

But I digress as I sit writing from a tiki bar along the Florida Keys. The Earth is rotating from a burning bundle of hydrogen and helium. Margaritas. Si.

Back to the story: The yellow school bus arrived at Walloon Lake. 10 cabins. Each cabin could sleep ten in the bedrooms, fold out couches, and to the drunk and stoned, the floor. While the skiers hit the slopes, the other Spartans prepared food, drank and had wild sex. After the day's skiing, arranged by the Lansing News, the 20 Spartans assembled in one cabin.

SPAGHETTI

The tables were pushed together for a Spartan feast. Appetizers were served along with a vat of Purple Jesus--grape juice, ice, floating fruit and hundred proof vodka in one cabin.

Jonathan Cooper, a rabbi's son, slipped in pure grain alcohol, which soon took effect. At Sean's request, the women only wore T shirts and panties. Some wore tennis shoes. I don't remember what the men wore. I wasn't looking...and the Purple Jesus set in.

After an hour of cocktails and appetizers, the Spartan crew sat down at the long table: massive unlimited salads (Olive Garden style), large bowls of delicious spaghetti and meatballs. Bread lushed with butter and garlic.

SPAGHETTI

All prepared by Harry, a former intel operative from Atsugi Air Base, Japan where a marine named Lee Harvey Oswald watched Race Car (a U2 spy plane) fly over the Soviet Union.

The army veteran, who had returned to State to finish his degree, knew exactly where Sean was headed. He also knew the fate of marine forward observers in combat ("Body Count," and "Body Count, continued," www.TriggerStreet.com).

When a marine requests support, we give it to him at Michigan State University. We also take care of soldiers when they return from duty. No post-traumatic stress disorder (PTSD) here.

SPAGHETTI

Candles lit the table. The stoned and hungry Spartans sat...but there was no silverware on the long table covered with a white tablecloth. Years of social etiquette had been programmed into the university students--but they were hungry and drunk...and what the hell...Sean Meehan was on his way to a combat zone.

There was no choice but to reach in with your bare hands and eat.

Now, I digress again to introduce a key player in the world of flying spaghetti.

Phil Mendershausen sat at the table and can cross validate the story I tell. He was a biochemistry Ph.D. candidate who also played rugby...a front line 220 lb. prop who would muscle the opposition for State.

His dissertation research involved lipids. Lipids cluster together in the blood stream as cholesterol. They clog the arteries and cause heart attacks.

At MSU, we not only party and fight; we also carry out important research to help vets and other citizens.

Phil would later in his professional life, run a blood lab the size of a football field that monitored blood chemistries at the VA.

I include his report in editing this important article in the party field of the behavioral sciences ("Ways to Prevent and Treat PTSD", a work in progress, "Fighting (what a marine does)," and "Basic Research on Lipids," in progress.

SPAGHETTI

Mendershausen: "As I remember, we sat down to eat, and I polished off at least one or two plates of spaghetti and sauce. There was bread too, flushed with butter.

"At some point I was faced with a third full plate of spaghetti covered with sauce. I remember holding it up and contemplating whether I could eat yet another plate full.

"Then, I looked to my left and there sat buxom Diana and I seem to recall the plate tilted somewhat and the sauced spaghetti slid to the side...and I sort of went with the moment.

"Reaching down with my left hand to grab the elastic on the front of her panties as my right hand holding the plate moved towards her buxom chest. For some inexplicable reason she was not objecting to what was going on. (Editor's note: remember the pure grain alcohol from Tom's Party Store, East Lansing.)

"Diana was well aware of me and the spaghetti...I just tilted the plate a little further and the full load hit her just below the belly button and slid down into the nest of her blonde bush...there to reside and give off its heat to an otherwise hot little pussy (Editor's note: science and good writing consist of detailed reporting.)

SPAGHETTI

"I let the elastic snap back and put my plate before me. Diana sat there...most people at the table saw what happened.

"I don't recall whether Diana got up or stayed seated, or what happened next. I do recall two spicy meatballs also slid into her panties."

But soon, the spaghetti began to fly: exactly what Sean had requested.

Shift the camera back to the author.

Diana slipped her hand under the white tablecloth and began to feel me up. She whispered in my ear, "You big, handsome Irishman...I'm going to take you home and fuck your brains out."

SPAGHETTI

As your writer fell to the floor in a drunken state...and then crawled under the table...I looked up at Diana, the goddess of the hunt, who later would transition into Dominatrix. (BAD ACTORS (Rev #5) www.TriggerStreet.com).

She was standing there stoned out of her mind in an MSU T shirt...she reached into the crotch of her silk panties and pulled out a handful of spaghetti.

Ah youth! There's nothing like it.

FADE OUT.

Story #3   **Body Count**

copyright 2012 James J. Moriarty, Jr.

Vietnam Memorial, Washington, D.C.

BODY COUNT

Synopsis: A marine forward observer counts "enemy bodies" after artillery barrages in Vietnam. Queer statistical information is reported to the Secretary of Defense. The public should be aware of false information as the U.S. moves into Afghanistan/Pakistan. M

Like Hemingway's Nick Adams' stories, I have a series of stories based on a good friend, Sean Meehan who was a forward observer in Vietnam.

As an early adolescent, Sean ran away from home. He put all his belongings in a red American Flyer wagon and walked one mile to my house. I thought, "Great, now I have a friend to play with whenever I want."

But my mom quickly called his mom, "the mother network," and Sean had to return home.

We both graduated from college in the Vietnam era. I went to a Big Ten graduate school to study psychology and statistics (I was deferred because the Pentagon knew soldiers would need psychological help).

Sean passed through Quantico for Officers' Candidate training. He was sent to Vietnam as a forward observer with an artillery unit. One of his tasks was to advance into the jungle after an artillery barrage and count "enemy" bodies.

BODY COUNT

The numbers were sent to the upper echelon of officers who forwarded the dead enemy count to the command. The numbers were sent to the Pentagon and Secretary of Defense Robert McNamara. McNamara then told the viewing audience on TV what was happening in Vietnam at a press conference.

Sean reported to me, he being the exception, that many of the forward observers inflated "enemy body counts"—often putting a log or a bundle of brush in the jungle into the count.

Now, I understand body counts are a difficult operation: mines, booby traps, plus snipers and ambushes. There are also wounded enemy soldiers waiting to take a last shot at an invading army. There's a lot of error.

I report these inflated body counts because while in grad school I would watch the nightly news as Secretary of Defense McNamara reported increasing "body counts" in Vietnam on national television.

As I studied statistics (means + standard deviations + analysis of variance + error measurements), I didn't know how the "enemy" could sustain the death rate that McNamara reported they were experiencing. Ultimately, two to

BODY COUNT 32

three million dead Vietnamese. 58 thousand Americans dead.

I report this information as the U.S goes deeper into "body counts" in the mountains of Afghanistan and Northwest Pakistan.

"False intelligence was used to drive the U.S. into Iraq the second time," Walter Cronkite, PBS.

Bill Moyers also reported on PBS that Italian Intelligence reported falsely to Britain and the U.S. about yellowcake uranium from Niger (May 4, 2007).

As THE SHERIFF, James Dickey, stated at the FADE OUT of Burt Reynolds' <u>DELIVERANCE</u> (1972).

"Dem boys is lying."

FADE OUT.

BODY COUNT 33

"Dem boyz is lying," JAMES DICKEY, the Sheriff at FADE OUT of <u>DELIVERANCE (1972)</u>.

Story #4   34

Body Count, Continued

copyright 2012 James J. Moriarty, Jr.

Synopsis: In the continuing Sean Meehan series, Meehan and Moriarty (M & M) salvage gold bars from the Gulf of Mexico. They melt it, drink beer and convert to cash in Vegas. Meehan, the marine forward observer Vet, looks back to Vietnam, and then to Afghanistan. M

National Cemetery, Arlington, Virginia

Sean Meehan, 65, asked me to join him in Key West, Florida for a little adventure and a chance to make some money. It was a "zero, sum" game: either we found sunken gold treasure, or we didn't.

He instructed me to meet him on the sunset side of the island at a marine basin where he had rented a yacht.

On board the "Risky Business," I met Sean and two ex-Navy frogmen. They were drinking Budweiser and exchanging war stories. Sean's stories were Vietnam era; the frogmen were young vets of the first Iraqi War. They had exercised their skills in the Persian Gulf. Someone had to turn off the oil valves before the Tomahawks were thrown into downtown Baghdad.

BODY COUNT, CONTINUED

As a forward observer in Vietnam, Sean maintained a long term relationship with the intelligence community. Over Argentine steak and American beer, an Air Force intel agent revealed to Sean that there were several sunken masses in the Gulf of Mexico that were not active subjects of the U.S. military.

The Air Force officer watched satellites for a living, and did not make mistakes. She concluded the masses were sunken Spanish galleons, possibly loaded with gold and silver from the New World. An ancient storm had probably driven the ships from the Caribbean to a grave in the Gulf. Their latitude and longitude placed them out of range of Florida's archaeological recovery law.

BODY COUNT, CONTINUED

As a footnote to history, because of American satellite surveillance, a modern fleet will never cross an ocean and create another Pearl Harbor.

As part of the deal, the frogmen were required to wear black spray painted sunglasses so that they did not learn the location of the wrecks they were about to explore.

As a childhood friend and land lover, I was not required to wear the special glasses. It was all blue water to me. I spent most of the ensuing venture sea sick, even with the help of Dramamine.

BODY COUNT, CONTINUED

All drinking stopped once we left port. This was serious, dangerous business, especially for the frogmen who would be deep underwater on a splintered wreck.

I won't reveal the latitude and longitude of the three shipwrecks because I never learned them.

And even if I did know the exact location, I would not inform the reader because we clearly did not get all the booty.

But we got a lot of it.

After a week of diving far from land, the two frogmen brought up three hundred ingots of gold with Spanish markings on them.

BODY COUNT, CONTINUED

At that point, the drinking began and the work stopped. We agreed not to be greedy and the frogmen were out of oxygen.

We sailed the yacht to New Orleans in time to drop the young men to Mardi Gras. Sean handed them each $10k in cash.

Sean and I then sailed to Galveston, Texas. I rented a U-Haul van and shopped Wal-Mart for Igloo coolers. Sean drank and protected the gold. We then transferred the bullion to the coolers and loaded them into the heavy duty van.
We returned the rented yacht and drove to Dallas.

We pulled the van into the double garage of a geologist friend. He set up shop so that we could melt the gold into ingots that are recognizable in this modern era.

We drank beer and melted gold.

As ingots cooled to room temperature, I brought them to various "cash for gold" shops that populate the Big D. No questions were asked in the vigorous cowboy economy.

We gave the geologist two of the original Spanish ingots and drove the van loaded with cash to Las Vegas. We checked into five high end hotels that featured poker rooms with safe deposit boxes for gamblers.

While one man protected the cash with concealed weapons, the other partner filled the boxes to the limit without drawing attention.

BODY COUNT, CONTINUED

We returned the van to U-Haul and then spent a week, or, was it three weeks, recuperating from our adventure. When we had enough high end R & R, we emptied two of the deposit boxes, rented a Jaguar and drove to La Jolla, California.

Sean selected a block and stone townhouse that featured a marble deck with a penthouse. It overlooked the Pacific Ocean.

Sean paid $1million cash for the unit. The broker, an ex-Marine, smiled at the clean transaction and disappeared.

It was time for me to do the same.

I left Sean Meehan, my boyhood friend who now has gray hair, on the stone deck of his townhouse.

BODY COUNT, CONTINUED

He was watching CNN news on his HD television. He also monitored an Android.

On the floor next to his white leather armchair were the Washington Post, the New York Times, the Chicago Tribune and Rolling Stone magazine.

He was drinking Budweiser beer from a pilsner glass.

As the sun set, he was looking at a modern map of Vietnam. He circled with a black magic marker the northwest quadrant of Ho Chi Minh City (formerly Saigon) and the location of the War Crimes Museum.

But I know his mind was on the killing fields of Afghanistan/Pakistan...and the reports of body counts in the mountains.

BODY COUNT, CONTINUED   44

I left Sean to return to my Hemingway writer's life style in the Florida Keys.

FADE OUT.

STORY #5

Gold in Key Largo

copyright 2012 James J. Moriarty, Jr.

Synopsis: Meehan, a Federal Agent, stops a hip hop gang from stealing gold from South Africans. Designed as a teleplay.

My life time friend, Sean Meehan, is a career federal agent. After a stint in the Marine Corps, Vietnam era, he signed on as an FBI Special Agent.

His successful career was tough on his marriage, although he did produce three children and several mortgages as the bureau moved him about the country looking for bad actors.

In 2000, his wife left him. Her lawyer made sure she got the benefits of being a bureau wife. To sooth his emotional wounds, Sean decided to take an extended "leave of absence" for six months following the divorce in New York City.

The bureau doesn't mind. It has plenty of white males to spare. The "leave of absence" helps it fill the Affirmative Action quotas following Congress' mandate.

GOLD IN KEY LARGO

Meehan decides to set up camp on the Risky Business, an idle yacht owned by a friend, a Wall Street banker who was too busy making money to use it.

The yacht is docked in Key Largo, the first key in the chain of small islands that dot the southern tip of Florida. The ocean going boat is moored at the end of Ocean Drive, on the Atlantic side of a long concrete channel.

Sean finally gets a chance to read the books and watch the DVDs he missed while chasing "bad actors" around the country. He even gets time to interact with his grown children who are starting families of their own.

His book choices are easy to understand: <u>The Warren Commission Report, 24 Volumes</u> (1964), with specific emphasis on volume 22, the evidence.

He also reads <u>The House Select Committee Final Assassinations Report, 12 volumes</u> (1979).

The DVDs are the Oliver Stone film, <u>JFK</u> (1991) and the various DVDs produced by the television networks on the events of Dealey Plaza, Dallas, Texas (November 22, 1963).

Peter Jennings (ABC News, 2003) is probably the best and most current. And then, the material produced by many authors including, <u>Case Closed</u> (1993), Gerald Posner.

C SPAN, History 3, updates historical work from November 22, 1963.

The HISTORY CHANNEL broadcasts continuing updates with ongoing work by historians on the events of November 22, 1963.

In the mist of a spring night, an ocean going yacht from South Africa docks at the small repair facility at the end of Ocean Drive. It is less than thirty yards from the Risky Business.

The following day, deeply tanned sailors from the South African yacht rent a Mercedes with one way tinted glass from the local Enterprise car rental agency. They leave one security officer to protect the yacht while they travel north to Miami.

Two men and a shapely blonde from the South African yacht drive downtown to Miami's business district, distinguished by its high rise steel and Plexiglas skyscrapers.

The South Africans drop the female sailor at a high end fashion boutique, and then visit an Italian men's tailor shop.

"Where are you from?" Enrico, 26, a young tailor inquires in a friendly manner.

"South Africa," they reply.

"What brings you to Miami?" Enrico asks intrusively.

"Gold," one man replies.

"Actually, it's none of your business, fag," the South African security officer snaps at the gay man. "Just tailor the suits!"

Enrico is no fool. He can tell by their ocean tans that these men have spent months at sea.

The fashionably dressed South African woman joins her two fellow sailors in her new outfit in the style of business Miami.

The three weathered sailors approve of one another's urban attire. They pay with a gold Amex card, and exit to their rented Mercedes.

Following his curiosity, and resenting the homophobic insult, Enrico follows them in a taxi.

The South Africans park their car in the underground garage of a building that houses an international bank known for its trading in precious metals and international currency.

Enrico drinks coffee in a Starbucks across the street from the bank. The South Africans reappear, smiling from their visit to the bank. They exit south in their rented Mercedes.

Enrico cell phones a hip hop gang that is nested in the in downtown Miami for the winter.

"I've got information for you," Enrico speaks softly into his cell phone. "South Africans have appeared in downtown Miami with ocean tans, and a visit to a precious metal bank."

"Come on, boy," the Brooklyn accent replies. "We're recouping from last night in South Beach."

Enrico taxis to one of the "beehives without bees," the massive high rises that have been built in Miami that have less than ten percent occupancy.

The landlord is glad to rent a luxury penthouse to a Brooklyn, New York "group" for the winter. Cash is paid in advance for the six month winter season.

Enrico pushes the speaker pad in the lobby of the building.

"It's gay Gucci," states Jackson, a young street punk from L.A. who attached himself to the gang. He shouts to the leader of the gang.

"Send him up," the leader replies.

The gang exchanges coke lines for the information that Enrico offers.

"These guys are bringing gold to Miami," Enrico shouts as he snorts several lines of cocaine.

"If it pans out, this brass box is yours," the leader points to a coffee table with a brass box full of white powder.

The sophisticated hip hop gang uses cell phones and ear buds to communicate.

The next day, they set up observation with Enrico at the Starbucks across from the precious metals trading bank.

A tattooed gang member waits near the underground parking lot of the gold bank. He waits for the return of the white Mercedes. He has an "electronic bird" in his ear.

Another gang member is ready in a rented black Mercedes, with one way solar protected glass.

The next day, the South Africans return to the bank in their white Mercedes. They park underground and enter the ground floor of the bank building.

"Communication" bristles among the gang from the parking lot lookout, to the driver, and, to the gang leader and Enrico nestled in Starbucks.

An hour later, the South Africans exit the gold trading bank.

The two Mercedes drive south by the magnificent estates of Cutler Ridge.

The South Africans arrive at Key Largo, unaware they are being followed.

The gang checks into the local Holiday Inn and sets up observation of the South African yacht.

Jackson, a gang member, goes fishing and carries out surveillance as Buck Wheat.

After the sun sets, all four of the South Africans go to an elegant dinner at Cocoanuts. They come back drunk.

The gang estimates they have two hours to pull the job the next time the South Africans go for a late night dinner.

The next evening, following sunset, all four South Africans head to a two hour dinner at Cocoanuts.

While one gang member monitors their evening dinner, the rest of the hip hop gang pull up to the yacht, and smash into the docked vessel.

"Smash and grab" is their style. It worked in the shopping malls of South Florida and pays for their "Snow Bird Winters."

Although their surveillance techniques were smooth, there is nothing smooth about their mode of "break and enter and smash and grab." Like MS 13, they have no hesitation to use brute force when necessary.

Unfortunately for the gang, Sean Meehan is watching their activities from the Risky Business. The loud "break and enter" style interrupts the evening news on CNN.

Meehan, an experienced law enforcement officer, cell phones 911, and tells the operator to call the Monroe County Police.

"A break in' is in progress," he speaks calmly. "A black gang of thieves has smashed into a docked yacht at the repair yard at the end of Ocean Drive on Key Largo. Send a full force of heavily armed men, now! This is FBI Special Agent Sean Meehan speaking."

Within a half hour, the Monroe County swat team arrives with two police cars, a van, and a black SUV.

he young driver of the gang's Mercedes is paralyzed with fear by the sudden appearance of the police. The leader of the gang and another hip hopper are arrested as they surrender from the yacht.

GOLD IN KEY LARGO

Meehan watches the developing scene from behind the one way windows of the Risky Business. He smiles.

The South Africans return from dinner to find the local police in complete control of the situation.

"We received a phone call from a good citizen," the Police Chief smiles.

After the police arrest the gang and leave the dock, Meehan walks over and introduces himself to the visitors from another continent.

"I was in the right place, at the right time," Meehan smiles.

The visitors thank him with a bottle of select Johannesburg wine and a bar of gold.

The moral of the story is: yes, the criminal element has their snitches, but the police have plenty of good citizens who hate crime, and help the police do their job.

FADE OUT.

Story #6

Vultures in Downtown Miami

copyright 2012 James J. Moriarty, Jr.

Synopsis: Real vultures fly around the Miami Dade courthouse. They serve as a metaphor for human vultures that circulate. Designed for a teleplay.

VULTURES

Vultures over Miami Courthouse

VULTURES

I always thought of vultures as a country/desert type of creature. I used to watch them eat dead deer on Old Georgetown Pike behind the headquarters of the Central Intelligence Agency, Langley, Virginia.

I had a brief stint with the agency as a contract officer. But because of my activities in rendition camps, the Department of Justice declared me "cruel and unusual." They told the CIA to drop me [cf. Screenplay BAD ACTORS (Rev #5) on KEVIN SPACEY'S www.TriggerStreet.com.]

I also saw vultures in John Wayne/Clint Eastwood movies, gathering around carrion in the desert. So I thought they were creatures of the sand.

VULTURES

My current work as a Federal Agent in the year 2010 brought me to downtown Miami. As I left the courthouse following a deposition on a Ponzi scheme out of Ft. Lauderdale, I saw about fifty vultures roosting on the block and stone Miami Dade Courthouse. The old structure has survived one hundred years of hurricanes.

Today, I write an additional story in the Sean Meehan collection: "Adventures of Sean and Me."

After Sean exited the Marine Corps, post-Vietnam, he was recruited into the FBI. He had nothing else to do, and the FBI liked to recruit ex Marines—they were in shape and easy to clear.

Their college and military records were always in order. Sean wanted to drag me into the FBI with the understanding we would be partners. I was a Big Ten educated psychologist who played rugby. I had no trouble throwing a man to the ground. Both traits are of value to the Bureau who now recruits more than lawyers and accountants, as in the old Hoover days.

The FBI agreed to clear the two micks as partners. Sean had intimate ties with the daughter of a top FBI official. I had dated the daughter of the head of general investigations. I was initially cleared in his living room while the daughter does whatever it is that adolescent women do before coming down the stairs for a date.

Sean and I grew up in Washington, D.C., a small town for the well connected.

I wasn't as easy to clear as Sean after my basic research into the properties of lysergic acid diethylamide 25, a specific isomer of LSD. It is a research drug from the Swiss laboratories of Sandoz. How's your Greek? It's a psycholytic pharmaceutical. Psychos = mind. lytos =relaxing drug. It's been misclassified as a hallucinogenic drug (Stanislov Grof, M.D. Realms of the Human Unconscious, 1975.)

The FBI is no fool: the behavioral science unit needs to know what the CIA's MK ULTRA project was all about. A psychologist is trained to answer such research questions.

They also want to know what are the sources of tons of cocaine that are being imported into the

VULTURES   67

U.S. They are interested in the criminal activity associated with the narcotic drug.

A criminologist can shed light on the sociology of such activity. Sean and I never bothered with the white powder. He preferred alcohol. I need to preserve my mucous membranes. I get flues in the winter. I had met a cocaine dealer who said, "My mucous membranes are just a memory." So I pass on coke. Holmes does not (BAD ACTORS #5, www.TriggerStreet.com).

But unless the DEA is lying to us, tons of the substance has been illegally imported into the U.S. for the past five decades [COCAINE COWBOYS (2006), THE MAN WHO MADE IT SNOW, a film in progress].

Anyway, I took a pass on the FBI early on, despite Sean's encouragement. They were more interested in Affirmative Action types, and females. I was more interested in the science of the Smithsonian Institution.

I studied evolution and the fundamental behavioral science question: why would a species of animal develop weapons that would destroy life on Earth. I even wrote an unproduced film script, <u>LOVE IN THE NUCLEAR AGE</u>, which dealt with this question.

Let's just say there was a vague time of "plausible deniability" in my career. Nothing illegal, immoral or fattening.

Or, you could say, there was time when I was "on loan," or acting as an "independent contractor" from one bureaucracy to another. Something vague like that. Sean continued as a Bureau agent; I pursued basic science.

I used my skills as a psychologist, statistician and series #7 (the stock broker exam) representative to earn a living.

After the stock market crashed from 13k to 7k, the Bureau decided to let me in the back door—post 9/11. Strings were pulled. Phone calls were made. Sean had a partner who packed the equipment and knew how to use it.

VULTURES

The FBI owed me that after discriminating against me and other white males with the promotion of women and affirmative action types.

Yes, Equal Opportunity makes a better Bureau and a fair society, but law enforcement still needs bad actors [cf. <u>BAD ACTORS (Rev #5)</u> www.TriggerStreet.com] like me.

Law enforcement requires men who can put a man up against the wall, handcuff 'em, and read them their rights. Muscle still has its place in the modern bureau.

Sean and I are well connected.

VULTURES

Let's not sidetrack on small details. I am here to write about the vultures and dead pigeons of the judicial center in downtown Miami.

The astute reader will note that I am writing metaphorically. The vultures in downtown Miami feed on the dead pigeons. The residents approve.

But there are also human vultures who prey on human stool pigeons who testify against organized crime. The feds do not approve. Hence we have the federal witness program.

VULTURES

After Sean's and my activities along Lincoln Road, South Beach at the Miami Models Agency (cf. BAD ACTORS (Rev #5) and the publication of "A REALLY EXPERIENCED Woman," (a short story on www.TriggerStreet.com), we were sent to the sweltering swamp of Florida's Everglades National Park.

The Park Rangers had noticed a suspicious gathering of 20+ vultures in the swamp.

I report our 120 degree field work in the Florida swamp because our "parallel team" who didn't tarnish the reputation of the bureau got to investigate fraud in the air conditioned high tech buildings that populate downtown Miami. Sean had seniority, but if you are a "bad boy," the bureau lets you know it.

VULTURES

Instead, two female agents, in smart white linen suits and low heels, were sent on the "air conditioned" assignment. They wore low heels in case they had to chase a "bad actor."

Both were good looking, well-tailored women. They wore Brooks Brothers suits when they interviewed people. The lead agent, Lucy Ploss, was a Marymount, Tarrytown, New York, graduate. She also had an MBA from the Wharton Business School, Philadelphia.

VULTURES 74

Initially, she worked for a Wall Street investment house, but became nervous when electronic files of mortgage backed securities didn't make sense. Her father was a Chief of Police on Long Island--so she had no trouble becoming a Special Agent in the FBI. She did have trouble in the pugil pits of Quantico during FBI training.

Her partner did not. Marylou Klick, her partner, a Georgia girl, had come up the hard way. She learned martial arts as well as street fighting in her Atlanta neighborhood of mixed races and ethnics.

After learning that the mathematics of engineering was too tough for her, Klick graduated from Georgia Tech with a business degree. She worked her way through an MBA program at Emory,

VULTURES

aka Coca Cola University. Klick, the sister of Nurse Klick (<u>BAD ACTORS (Rev #5)</u>, was another obsessive/compulsive type.

Whereas nurse Klick worked with young men and their sperm under a microscope, Agent Klick preferred the detailed numbers of spreadsheets. Klick liked to drink and fuck. But after she picked up an itch, she decided it was safer to stay home, drink and watch movies when she wasn't in the field.

I am reporting the type of women the bureau is recruiting these days: tailored and tough, as well as well educated.

VULTURES

Over drinks at a cop bar, I remember spilling a beer when Klick said she was embarrassed by the unethical business practices of her corporate executive colleagues. She had worked the corporate world after getting her MBA.

Many in the corporate world operate on the principle, "do whatever you can get away with."

Like Sean Meehan, I was Jesuit educated. Ethics and morals are an essential part of a Jesuit education. Evidently, Emory Business School thinks the same.

Because she thought that many business practices were not only unethical, but illegal, she became an FBI Special Agent. The two women were paired. Klick and Ploss. Ploss and Klick.

VULTURES

After "A REALLY EXPERIENCED Woman" (a short story on www.TriggerStreet.com) was first published, a frumpy government bureaucrat was flown to Miami first class to interview Sean and me.

"The Justice Department has to do something," Ms. Frances Firkins, a GS 9 from Firth, Florida, spoke firmly to us. "But you should know that after reading "A REALLY EXPERIENCED Woman", I learned a few tricks that my boyfriend appreciated," she smiled.

Firkins was a good sport. She had graduated first in her class at Florida State. Her father was the first mayor of Firth when it was first incorporated. You could say she was a member of the first family of Firth, a nice town in north Florida.

Sean, a Vietnam combat veteran, and I, a psychologist who had studied the Kinsey Report (1948 and 1953), The Human Sexual Response (Masters and Johnson, 1966), and The Lyndon B. Johnson's and Richard Nixon's Commission on Obscenity and Pornography (1970) prepared by an ex DIA (Defense Intelligence Agency) psychologist during the Nixon administration, smiled back across the steel desk.

"So I'll write a report and send it to your supervisor. Thank you. No more government time will be spent on this matter," Frances Firkins of Firth, Florida concluded.

VULTURES

The upshot was that a female rookie investigative team got the assignment to interview "persons of interest" in the air conditioned buildings of downtown Miami.

Sean and I were sent to sweat it out in the August heat of the Everglades National Park. We drove Route 41, the Tamiami trail, deep into the swamp: insects, humidity and a beautiful natural ecological system.

Just like downtown Miami, twenty plus vultures were circulating in the heat.

The park rangers had noted the unusual gathering, found a decaying corpse, and called the FBI.

VULTURES

It turns out the 20+ vultures were circling what was left of an alligator chewed corpse of what I suspected was a "human stool pigeon."

I report these facts because the astute reader should know that in real life, it ain't like what they report on "CSI, Miami." In real life, the bad actors delay capture, and often escape due process because there are human vultures that prey on stool pigeons aka federal witnesses.

VULTURES

In Virginia, we feel that "justice delayed, is justice denied." The feds don't work that way. Federal justice "grinds slowly, but exceedingly fine," as I read in a short story at Gonzaga, a Jesuit High School in the District of Columbia ("Another Admiral Rickover Story: Character." Story #10 in this collection. <u>Professor Moriarty's Short Stories (2012)</u>.

We slopped into the swamp and found what was left of a male corpse. The alligators had eaten large chunks of the body. The vultures had plucked out the eyeballs—evidently the first thing a bird of prey does.

There was no attempt to hide the body. Unknown suspects probably took the live subject into the swamp to get what information they could

VULTURES

from the "stool pigeon." That is, they wanted to know what he had revealed to federal prosecutors.

I couldn't tell if the murder was done day or night, or even if the subject was still alive when the alligators started to chew. Forensics handles those details.

I suspect it was the work of MS 13, a Latino gang out of San Salvador, then Dallas, Los Angeles, and Arlington and Roanoke, Virginia. In 2008, they stabbed a pregnant female stool pigeon to death in the Shenandoah Valley of western Virginia.

VULTURES

I doubt that MS 13 operates in the Plexiglas and steel buildings of downtown Miami. But their services may have been contracted to carry out the hit on a stool pigeon. We cell phoned the forensic team and perspired in the 120 degree heat.

The forensic team photographed the body and surroundings with digital film. They indicated an unknown cause of death—only the forensic lab could make further diagnosis.

As I watched the forensic team scoop up the putrid remains of the corpse, I looked into the sky of the August sun. I began to think the morale of the story is: if you're going to rat out organized crime--you got to be aware there are human vultures who circulate around the judicial process.

VULTURES 84

Real life doesn't wrap up neat and clean like "New York: Law and Order."

Sean, using his Irish charm, plus his seniority, asked the rubber gloved forensic pathologist to show us the IPhone that the male body clutched in his left hand.

The pathologist wiped the swamp slime off the screen, pressed the iPhone on, and up came a series of equations.

From my days as a psychologist/statistician and a Series #7 AMEX Account Representative, I recognized what was on the screen: derivative equations that are used on Wall Street to value mortgage backed securities, REITS (Real

Estate Investment Trusts), and faux mortgage backed securities & legal settlements...and SWAPS.

I suspect that we were looking at the body of an accountant.

FADE OUT.

An Experienced Woman

copyright 2012 James J. Moriarty, Jr.

Meehan and Moriarty (M & M) drink at Finnegan's Wake (James Joyce), Lincoln Road, South Beach, Miami. Moriarty collects material for a screenplay <u>BAD ACTORS (Rev #5)</u>. Sean Meehan asks Moriarty if he knows what an "experienced woman is like?"

AN EXPERIENCED WOMAN

AN EXPERIENCED WOMAN

Sean Meehan and I liked to hang out along Lincoln Road, South Beach, Miami. I would gather material for <u>BAD ACTORS (Rev #5)</u> on Kevin Spacey's website www.TriggerStreet.com.

Sean would drink.

After an excellent meal at the Meat Market, we crossed the trendy avenue to Finnegan's Wake (James Joyce) for drinks. Sean, of Scot Irish descent, ordered Johnnie Walker scotch. I, the son of a BIC (Bronx Irish Catholic), preferred Jameson Irish whiskey on the rocks.

I was staring at the models that walk Lincoln Road in their high heel shoes, short skirts and Miami heat cleavage. After his second drink, Sean asked me,

AN EXPERIENCED WOMAN

"Jim, how do you know when a woman is experienced?"

I had no reply.

Sean, a man of the world, stated, "When a woman comes up to you...smiles, looks you in the eye...then turns around...bends over, flips up her dress, and reveals that she is only wearing garter belts.

I laughed.

Sean, a Vietnam Vet, ordered his third scotch.

"How do you know when a woman is REALLY EXPERIENCED?" he continued.

"I don't know," I replied.

                                                FADE OUT.

A REALLY Experienced Woman

copyright 2012 James J. Moriarty, Jr.

Meehan & Moriarty (M&M), in a continuing series of short stories, move their set to South Beach, Miami. They are going to interview DOMINATRIX, a woman both men had an affair with years ago. Her name appeared on the iPhone of an accountant who was chewed to death by alligators in the Everglades swamp.

A REALLY EXPERIENCED WOMAN

"THE NEXT WHISKEY BAR"

A REALLY EXPERIENCED WOMAN

In the continuing Meehan and Moriarty (M & M) short stories series, I last left the two federal agents drinking Johnnie Walker scotch and Jameson Irish whiskey at Finnegan's Wake (James Joyce) on Lincoln Road, South Beach, Miami ("An Experienced Woman," www.TriggerStreet.com).

They have now moved down Lincoln Road to The Next Whiskey Bar (The Doors).

The two men were discussing what an experienced woman is like...the kind of woman with whom a man likes to share a bed...a woman who likes and enjoys sex, not just going along with what a woman is expected to do.

A REALLY EXPERIENCED WOMAN

DOMINATRIX is such a woman. She selects a man she finds attractive and invites him to her bed.

In real life, Dominatrix is PAMELA KNIGHT, the Director of the Miami Models Agency (Knight, known to the intel agencies, and to an ARAB SHEIK, as Dominatrix appears as the lead actress in the unproduced screenplay BAD ACTORS (Rev #5), www.TriggerStreeet.com).

When she is not running the "cat walk," she contracts her services, and that of "select" models to the intel agencies (Amazonia, Brazil. Xman, the Persian Gulf. the Ruhr Valley, et al.) and the Justice Department (tracking Bernie Madoff), and to private entities (RAND Corporation, "Wikileak: Baja, the

51st. State," www.TriggerStreet.Com and to Wall Street firms et al.)

On request, I describe what A REALLY EXPERIENCED woman is like.

Meehan, sipping his second Johnnie Walker, asks, "Moriarty, now that you know what an experienced woman is like, do you know what A REALLY EXPERIENCED woman is like?"

Moriarty smiled, "No, tell me, agent Meehan!"

Meehan smiled as he looked into the glass mirror behind the bar.

"A REALLY EXPERIENCED woman comes up to you...smiles in your face...turns around...bends over...reveals she is only wearing garter belts...she spreads her cheeks...opens her mouth...and says with pleasure...'pick a hole' and enjoy a free unlimited buffet."

I ordered my second Jameson whiskey.

I know how Dominatrix operated.

When I was a graduate student at Michigan State--she felt me up under the white clothed table at a ski weekend at Walloon Lake, Michigan ("Spaghetti in the Panties," www.TriggerStreet.com).

She also made Lt. Sean Meehan, USMC stand up and salute her before he headed to Vietnam as a forward observer. "Come back, marine, with your shield, not on it." ("A Modern Spartan Woman," www.TriggerStreet.com).

A REALLY EXPERIENCED WOMAN

We both knew we would have to interview her as part of a federal investigation into the corpse that was found in the Everglades swamp, a federal property ("Vultures in Downtown Miami," www.TriggerStreet.com).

The iPhone of the alligator chewed accountant had not only included a chain of financial equations with math models of derivatives, option positions and mortgage backed securities, it also contained the name of Dominatrix's front operation, The Miami Models Agency.

Forget the scotch and whiskey...and even the murder investigation.

A REALLY EXPERIENCED WOMAN   98

We both were interested in Dominatrix as a sex object...and curious about which one she would choose.   FADE OUT.

Alcoholism and Recovery in the Keys

copyright 2012 James J. Moriarty, Jr.

Synopsis: Birds and humans recover from harm in the Florida Keys. Alcoholism, oil and war are discussed.

ALCOHOLISM

ALCOHOLISM

Following the "Vultures in Downtown Miami" incident (www.TriggerStreet.com), Sean Meehan and I decided to take a break. The case would not be solved in the Everglades swamp where an alligator chewed an accountant to death.

Our parallel Federal team, Klick and Ploss, Ploss and Klick, would work the investigation to the next level in the Plexiglas and steel buildings in downtown Miami.

The team of two tough agents, an ex-Marine and a former rugby prop, needed some R & R. We headed south to the Florida Keys. I drove. Meehan drank. Sean liked to wear his lucky Michigan State tee shirt and his camouflage Marine shorts…and sip Budweiser.

As you drive south in the Keys, you first hit Key Largo. The movie, KEY LARGO (1948), was filmed there. The song "Bogie and Bacall" told the story a generation later. The film featured a bad actor, Edgar G. Robinson, as good an antagonist as it gets.

You drive past the Marriott Resort on the right, and then the Hilton Resort comes up fast at fifty mph. I suggest you stop for a leisurely lunch on the Hilton's third floor restaurant—the food is average, but the view of the Gulf of Mexico is spectacular.

The Hilton puts you on alert for the Florida Keys Wild Bird Center (www.FKWBC.org), Tavernier. It's one mile south of the Hilton. The

ALCOHOLISM

sanctuary heals injured birds. It features two pairs of red eyed hawks---prey does not go down easy to predators. Prey fight back.

You can walk the catwalk to the shore's edge. There you find black vultures nesting in the tree tops, intimidating if you are a dying animal.

But today, I write about the feeding of injured pelicans---some two hundred birds who gather at 3:30 pm for a daily feast of frozen fish and squid.

I talked with the woman who created the sanctuary. She's a senior citizen who migrated to the Keys some twenty years ago. I asked her why she came to this rich ecological niche.

"Alcoholism," she replied.

I didn't ask her if she was escaping it, or practicing it. It's prevalent in American Society---a slow disease that addicts you physiologically in ten years (after James F. Rooney, Ph.D. Sociology, Fulbright Professor at Penn State.) Nicotine grabs you in six months (Rooney continued).

But alcoholism is more than a social problem. "Come on, have another drink." After a while the cells and tissue of your body demand it. Just like the wounded birds that have humans who nurture them back to health, humans have doctors, nurses and other caregivers who "have mercy."

These professionals bring substance abusers back to health. But you got to have enough sense to ask for help. You got to ask for help before the toxicity principle asserts itself.

Treatment may come from the medical technician who drips valium into the patient so that delirium tremens (DTs) do not kill the alcoholic during alcohol withdrawal. Or, it may be the psychotherapists who vent anger and other emotions from their clients.

Or, it may be other recovering alcoholics at "meetings" who support them in their effort to return to sobriety.

Anyway, the senior citizen who ran the sanctuary, then asked me, "Why are we at war?"

"9/11," I quickly replied. "The United States was attacked with cunning and full malice. The World Trade Center was erased and three thousand people were killed in less than an hour. Terrorists were trained in camps in Afghanistan. They learned to fly in South Florida and Laurel, Maryland. The Pentagon was attacked as well."

"I understand," she replied. "But it's really about oil, isn't it?"

"Yes, there is oil and titanium in Afghanistan," I stated.

"Soldiers are dying," the senior citizen continued. "We need other sources of energy.... solar and wind."

I picked some fleas from her dog. I knew that solar has not worked because there is no way to store the energy. But physicists and engineers are working on the technical problem.

I then smiled as I watched the men with rubber gloves and boots feed pelicans who had trouble fishing on their own.

The senior left the shore's edge as the earth rotated away from the sun's light.

I returned to the Hummer that we had rented.

Meehan was in the front seat, drinking…mumbling about "body counts in Vietnam and Afghanistan (cf., "Body Count," and "Body Count, continued", on www.TriggerStreet.com .)

ALCOHOLISM

We drove away in our gasoline powered vehicle like millions of other motorists. We headed south to Key West where drinking is an art.

The End.

Story #10

Another Admiral Rickover Story: Character

copyright 2012 James J. Moriarty, Jr.

Admiral Hyman Rickover, head of the Nuclear Navy, needs a cab ride in the spring rain of Washington, D.C. Sean Meehan, the son of a Navy Captain, gives it to him and learns about his father's relation to the Admiral.

"You're the only man to call me a son-of-a-bitch to my face." Like father, like son. Sean is my partner as a Federal Agent.

CHARACTER

Synopsis: Character counts in the Nuclear Navy and the playing fields of the nation's capital, Washington, D.C.

CHARACTER

Like father, like son. In the continuing Sean Meehan series of stories, I write today about the character of my partner's father.

Sean Meehan and I were educated at Gonzaga College High School, a Jesuit prep school in the District of Columbia. Ethics and morals were taught and lived there daily. We were educated rigorously in science and the arts.

Each day after class, Meehan played sports until 5:00 pm. He then drove his father's car across town to a complex of government buildings where he picked up his father, a high level federal government executive.

During World War II, Mr. Meehan was in Naval Intelligence. His job was to follow an ambitious, aggressive naval officer who was "out to make a name for himself": Hyman Rickover.

The war was coming to an end in the Pacific. Too many sailors had died. The Navy anticipated the Cold War and the role nuclear weapons would play in it. The high command did not want Rickover to engage in risky actions. So it ordered Meehan to follow Rickover around, and report his activities to the Pentagon.

That's the "back story" as they say in screenplay writing.

Today's story is written about an incident in the spring of 1962. The Cuban Missile Crisis was six months away. It was raining hard in downtown Washington, D.C. You could not get a cab. Mr.

Meehan didn't need one. He had a son on whom he could count.

Sean picked up his father, an engineer, at the Nuclear Regulatory Commission. The father always sat in the back seat and monitored his seventeen year old son's driving. Never an accident.

At Connecticut and K Street, Northwest, now the home of multiple high power lobbying firms, Mr. Meehan saw Admiral Rickover, head of the Nuclear Navy, trying to hail a cab.

"Pull over," Meehan mumbled to his son.

Admiral Rickover looked into the car. He recognized Captain Meehan. He opened the front door of the car and sat down. The heavy spring rain continued. Neither man spoke.

Sean drove K Street to Washington Circle, home of the George Washington University Engineers where nuclear engineering is taught.

"Stop here," the Admiral grumped.

He stepped out of the car…got ready to slam the door shut…then leaned into the back seat…looked Captain Meehan in the eye and said, "You're the only man to call me a son-of-a-bitch to my face."

He slammed the car door, and walked into the rain to teach nuclear engineering to Naval Officers. These officers are men who don't back down. I know… because I used to play rugby with them on the mall of the nation's capital.   My partner, Sean Meehan, has the same character his father had.

The End.

Wikileak: BAJA, the 51st State

copyright 2012 James J. Moriarty, Jr.

Synopsis: A Marine expeditionary force will take over the Baja. The State Department will work a "debt for land" swap with the Mexicans. Hummers & government owned GM refrigerators will be offered as part of the deal. Satire.

WIKILEAK: BAJA

I am writing this Wikileak Report with extreme apprehension. I know it will result in a visit from the DIA...then the FBI...and finally a hearing at the House Foreign Relations Committee on Capitol Hill.

I will be sworn in, and forced to reveal the truth about an ongoing top secret Government report that I have been editing for the past five years.

The program involves cooperation between the Pentagon, the State Department, and of course, the current White House.

To be brief: the essence of the program is that an expeditionary force of United States Marines from Camp Pendleton, Southern California will carry out maneuvers along the Mexican Baja peninsula.

WIKILEAK: BAJA

The Mexican government will be told the Marines are merely carrying out an exercise in case they have to invade a Middle Eastern sand based emirate.

In fact, they will take over the Mexican Baja from Tijuana down to the arid tip of the peninsula.

The expeditionary force will land on all the beaches that can be taken from the water: the Pacific Ocean and the Sea of Cortez.

Once the Marines have taken control of the peninsula, the State Department will inform the Mexican government that they should accept a "land for debt" swap.

Mexican debt to the U.S. will be wiped out in the deal.

If the Mexicans do not immediately agree to the offer, refrigerators and GM cars from Detroit will be added to the deal. These assets are properties that the U.S. Government has acquired by its partialtakeover of the auto industry. Hummers are designed for the sandy peninsula.

Corporations such as Taco Bell, Hilton and Marriott Resorts, will be offered prime development sites featuring beachfront property. Taco Bell, Moe's Southwest, and Carlos & Charlie's will show the Mexicans how to make food that does not produce "tourista."

WIKILEAK: BAJA

Campgrounds like KOA, hostels and low cost motel systems like Motel 6, will be offered less desirable sites, but will be welcomed for the working family and the unemployed who continue to plague the economy at ten per cent.

Unemployed Mexicans will find plenty of work as the Baja evolves into the 51st American state. They will help in establishing the engineering system that will plumb water from the Sierra Mountains into the Baja.

WIKILEAK: BAJA

Corporations such as Taco Bell, Hilton and Marriott Resorts, will be offered prime development sites featuring beachfront property. Taco Bell, Moe's Southwest, and Carlos & Charlie's will show the Mexicans how to make food that does not produce "tourista."

Wind mills will produce electricity along with extensive solar panel systems. The drug cartels, Mexican & non Mexican, can invest their extensive cash holdings on Wall Street to finance projects known as REITS (Real Estate Investment Trusts).

Hell, why not make drugs legal in the 51st state? See if the new tax base works, or, if anybody wants to work in a drug induced state?

Think of all the new beach front property that developers can work on?

Now that the secret program has been revealed through WikiLeaks, we can begin open negotiations with modern Mexico.

It's good for their debt ridden economy, and it expands the United States.

"Land for debt. Debt for land."

Let the new world order take place. Thanks, Mr. Bush, senior.

The End.

Blanketing a Homosexual

copyright 2012 James J. Moriarty, Jr.

Summary: Semi-fiction.

Inappropriate homosexual advances in a shower room disrupt unity in a military operation. The Sergeant decides that supporting the Marines at Khe Sahn trumps due process.

BLANKETING 123

BLANKETING 124

BLANKETING

The following story is based on true events. The details are fuzzy because the writer was not present---so let's just call it "semi-fiction."

During the Vietnam War, an Air Force unit in Thailand was charged with loading bombs onto B-52s that would fly over North Vietnam and help bomb it into the Stone Age.

BLANKETING

A military unit must work together in a smooth operation---each man doing his job with precision and in conjunction with the unit.

Bombs load carefully. The plane is fueled. Mechanical and engineering systems are tuned. The airmen may not like one another personally, but cooperation is essential.

What happens in the shower room can affect the way a unit loads its bombs on a plane. One of the unit's members was a homosexual who liked to look at the genitals of other members of the unit in the shower room.

BLANKETING

Heterosexual men---military or otherwise---don't want other men looking at their private parts. And they don't want other men feeling them up, or commenting on their personals. And they certainly don't want to be felt up or slapped on the ass.

One of the unit members violated that unwritten code. Not once, not twice but at least one too many times.

The writer wasn't in the shower when it happened, but...the astute reader can figure it out.

You don't feel another man's butt when it's not welcome.

BLANKETING

At night, while the unit's sergeant slept, several soldiers "blanketed" the offending member. If the reader needs a visualization of "blanketing," watch Stanley Kubrick's <u>FULL METAL JACKET</u> (1987). Vincent d'Onofrio was not a smooth functioning member of his unit. He paid the price under a blanket at night.

Back to our story on an Air Force base in Thailand during the Vietnam War.

The sergeant's job was to keep a smooth running unit who loaded planes that bombed North Vietnam Regulars who were attacking Marines from the jungle to the east of Khe Sanh Jan 21- Jul 9,

BLANKETING

1968. The Marines were human bait (The History Channel). The operation was run directly from the White House through the Pentagon.

The sergeant could not let an incident that occurred in the shower disrupt unit morale.

A blanket was placed over the homosexual who had violated the shower code...he was beaten with fists and probably pieces of wood and metal.

The sergeant rolled over in his sleep and kept snoring.

The offending unit member was then thrown out a second story window. Bones were broken. The next day, he was admitted to the base hospital. He was treated and given a medical discharge from the United States Air Force.

There may have been a crime committed! Was the crime making unwelcome advances in the shower room? or, the punishment that was inflicted on the unwanted homosexual advances?

"Don't ask. Don't tell."

FADE OUT.

HELP: Big, Black Women

copyright 2012 James J. Moriarty, Jr.

Synopsis: Big, black women are the cornerstones of American society. They are there when you need them.

"Chain…chain…chain." Aretha Franklin

HELP

The reader knows them. You've seen them all about the world in which we live: Big, Black Women. They are the cornerstones of American Society. They help us all when we need them.

An example of their service: the writer was "snow birding" in Miami one winter. The city of Miami recognizes and rewards Senior Citizens who make it to their twilight years.

One benefit: seniors ride the bus for free. The taxpayers foot the bill.

The bus driver was a big, black woman about age 40. Her muscles and girth showed through her freshly laundered uniform.

The driver pulled to a bus stop and placed the vehicle in park.

She then rearranged some gear that is part of the bus' design at the front of the bus and lifted a heavy metal frame.

She pulled a lever which leveled the front steps of the bus to the curb. She stepped down to the curb to a waiting Senior Citizen in a mechanized wheelchair.

The driver pushed the wheelchair onto the ramp and pulled a lever which allowed the senior's wheelchair to rise onto the bus' platform which had been designed to clamp the wheelchair into a safe place.

The forty plus passengers waited patiently and watched as the five minute procedure took place. The driver then closed the bus' door and

HELP

nodded to the senior that the engineered procedure was safely completed.

She then pushed the transmission to drive, and we drove into the rush hour traffic.

As a man who has recently qualified as a senior, but not a wheel chaired senior, I thought, "I hope that driver is around when my time comes."

Another example of the small, but key role that a Big, Black Woman has played in this writer's life is an unknown woman who worked the front desk at a Washington, D.C. FEDEX office on Capitol Hill.

It was 10:00 pm when most printing facilities are closed.

This writer ran into the FEDEX office in a panic. I had a deadline for a Word Document.

HELP

"We don't do that here, but go ten blocks to the FEDEX office at the Eastern Market," she calmly stated easing my panicked state. "It's open 24/7 and the people will help you there."

I smiled and followed her directions. Small, but key directions in a moment of panic from a Big, Black Woman.

Now we move underground to the District of Columbia's Metro system.

This aging writer was taking his annual escape south on the Amtrak from Union Station. I had six athletic bags and luggage packed tight for the winter. Too many bags for a senior to carry comfortably.

HELP

I dropped an overloaded bag and it broke open. A young black woman who was a Metro sanitation worker asked, "You need help?"

"As much help as I can get these days," I half smiled, but also knew I couldn't do it alone.

She gave me two heavy duty plastic trash bags, packed me up, and the senior was on his way to Union Station and the Amtrak, south.

Speaking of escaping cold winters and heading south, I have a friend who is homeless---he also has mental problems which probably does not make him the type of person to share a house.

The winter of 2010 was characterized as "bitter cold" in the Washington, D.C. area and elsewhere.

HELP

My friend, who we will call Harry, was living outdoors. He doesn't like the homeless shelters because other men bully him. He must sleep with his laptop and shoes on his chest. Thieves operate in the shelters.

But the winter of 2010 was too tough. I had escaped to the Florida Keys and was writing "Gold in Key Largo," "Alcoholism and Recovery in the Keys," and "Vultures in Downtown Miami." (www.TriggerStreet.com)

I could do nothing for Harry---except receive a phone call from his hospital bed.

Harry had barely made it onto an Arlington County bus and walked into the Emergency Room at The Virginia Hospital Center.

HELP

When he woke up in a hospital bed, both his kidneys were gone. A black female medical social worker was standing at his side.

She provided help to the 50 year old man through the Social Security system. He now has a two room apartment in an attic and some financial support. But his two kidneys are gone.

For two years, I provided him transportation to the DaVita Dialysis Centers in the Washington, D.C. metropolitan area.

One day he had a mental breakdown when I picked him up. Harry shouted,

"The baboons that run the clinic entered the wrong data."

HELP

While driving him in 35 mph traffic in downtown Fairfax, Virginia, Harry punched me. Psychologists call it "displacement of anger."

But that is another story.

I write today about the black female social worker who got him housing and financial assistance. You know the type. Black Women who are there when you need them.

I'll close out the story by writing about the Big, Black Woman who was married to one of my best friends, J.R. She is now deceased.

J.R. is a retired Air Force Sergeant whose idea of a good time is to go to the gym at Andrews Air Base, Maryland and pump iron. Sometimes he has to look an enlisted man in the eye and set the situation straight. The muscle in his arms transforms into his firm speech.

Now, back to his wife, a muscled Big, Black Woman who was a career matron at the D.C. jail. Paula could put a prisoner up against the wall, handcuff her and tell the prisoner what her rights are.

Sometimes, Paula would invite me to church services where other black women and she wore white lace with their Sunday Best.

I would give her a hug and a kiss on her cheek, and know that I was "welcome" as one of the few white guys at the service.

By now, I know the reader is aware of the type of woman I am describing.

HELP

They are the cornerstones of American Society. When you need "help," don't be afraid to ask. They are highly competent and they get the job done right.

When they don't know what to do, they tell you, "No, Miss Scarlett, I don't know nothing about having babies" (Missy in <u>GONE WITH THE WIND</u>, 1937).

But most of time, the big, black nurse at your hospital bedside, or the voice on the phone at Police Headquarters, or the social worker who determines what your benefits are, is highly competent and gets it right.

With the coming Presidential elections of 2012, I sometimes wonder if the Republican Party will integrate them into the infrastructure of its extensive political organization?

HELP

The Democrats certainly do, and it makes for a better society.

"Chain, chain, chain..." Aretha Franklin.

Big, Black Women know how and who to help. I know who they are.

So does the District of Columbia's Metro, FEDEX, and the Women's Prison...Amtrak, the Miami Transit System, Arlington's Virginia Hospital Center.

American society relies on them---they are like a sorority. None of the women I mentioned know one another, or even know that this scribe has written about them.

In the world of film/theatre, they are known as "good actors."

I know them. I appreciate their performances.

I suggest the astute reader gets to know them. They will improve the quality of your life.

FADE OUT.

Story #14

Research and Prayer

copyright 2012 James J. Moriarty, Jr.

an essay + short story

Model of DNA

RESEARCH

Synopsis: Science and modern medicine are the way to go for human health...but research indicates that prayer has its place in medicine.

James Moriarty

HR Dept

Test@Academia-Research.com

20 April 2012

"There is no hope for doing perfect research" (Griffiths, 1998, p.97 available on a Google search).

Let's not be pedantic. As Griffiths, a Harvard trained physicist, defines the term "research," he is correct. Science is not in the profession of "perfection." But it does want to get it right within a small variation margin of error.

"For every ongoing research we either see two views or we see that current research unravels something that an earlier research did not or it might defy an existing belief that shocks many," (Griffiths, 1998).

The scientific method is an ongoing process. Scientists carry out an experiment, publish their methodology and expect other scientists to replicate their methods and find the same conclusion.

If the same methodology does not produce the same results, there is a problem.

To illustrate this principle, one scientist interviewed on the television program "Sixty Minutes" stated with humor, "The non-football playing schools could not replicate the fusion experiments carried out in football playing universities (n.d.)."

Keeping our two page discussion to scientific research, as opposed to historical or literary research, Wikipedia states, "research is the systematic investigation into existing or new knowledge. It is used to establish or confirm facts, reaffirm the results of previous work, solve new or existing problems, support theorems, or develop new theories."

The peer review system keeps the quality of scientific work strong; fraud and inaccuracies are kept out of the stream of good science.

For example, Watson and Crick (Nature, 1953) used models based on the hard data of Rosalind Franklin to determine that Linus Pauling was wrong in his research that stated "the DNA helix is a triple structure."

Franklin's empirical use of X-Ray crystallography and diffraction data indicates the structure is a double helix (Wikipedia).

When a psychologist states that an individual is smart, he does not have to know the exact IQ of the subject. But he does have to be within a five percent variation. "Perfection" is not necessary. No need to do "perfect research." A small range of error is acceptable. We just want to admit the smartest students to a physics graduate program or to medical school.

RESEARCH

It takes superior brain power to carry out "perfect research" with "logical empiricism." Does it make sense? Can we test it? Can the results be replicated by other labs with small variation? -- Written with humor and imagination by Professor Moriarty from the Epcot Center, Disney World.

I submitted the above two page essay to Academia-Research.com in the process of applying for an online writing job.

I hope the reader appreciates science as the article will push his cognitive understanding of the scientific method.

The reader should know that I understand MLA, OWL, Purdue and the APA writing style...and I can write.

The astute reader can also determine that I am a logical empiricist: if I cannot measure it and make logical sense of the phenomenon, I'm not interested in it.

I state the above point of view, although I was educated in the Catholic school system--a good place to learn ethics and morals. Nuns taught me to read, write and do arithmetic (St Rita's School, Alexandria, VA, 1958). Jesuits prepped me for college with science, mathematics and the humanities (Gonzaga High School, Washington, D.C., 1962).

I also studied science and math, languages and the humanities at a Jesuit college (Holy Cross College, Worcester, MA, 1966).

RESEARCH

Harvard and Georgetown Universities advanced my knowledge of the behavioral science in summer school sessions (1963-65).

Self-study at the Smithsonian Institution also educated me. Evolution was not part of the Catholic curriculum. I don't know if the faculty did not know about it, or they suppressed knowledge of evolution.

Using the scientific method, the Museum of Natural History clearly demonstrates that humans are the product of two million years of primate development; and modern civilization is about 10,000 years old.

While in graduate school at Michigan State, I read a small paper by Sigmund Freud titled, "The Future of an Illusion" (1927).

RESEARCH

Freud (1927) developed the concepts of the Unconscious, Pre Consciousness, and Consciousness (The New Introductory Lectures).

In "An Illusion," he suggested that the concept of "God," is a universal concept among humans. It comes from a mothering/fathering figure that holds an infant in their arms and nurses them--especially when an infant cries.

That's the "backstory" as they say in screenwriting.

Today, I visited a friend who is a patient at the Seventh Day Adventist Hospital, Celebration, Florida-- three miles from Disney World's gates.

Celebration is an artificial town built with the many architectural styles that the U.S.A. has. Disney created it for its employees.

The Celebration Hospital is state of the art design architecturally.

I can't evaluate how good the hospital staff is--- I leave that to the Florida Hospital Board. But I bet it's real good.

The surgical unit features the Da Vinci surgical robot. It trains surgeons in its use. The Da Vinci was originally developed so that a surgeon in Manhattan could assist a military surgeon in Afghanistan operate "remotely" on a wounded soldier. (PowerPoint presentation at Florida's Osceola Regional Hospital, 2012).

Anyway, to follow Freud's insight, this logical positivist empiricist, has always regarded prayer as a form of superstition...a placebo.

Psychiatrically, it would be called a "parataxic behavior "(Harry Stack Sullivan, <u>The Interpersonal Theory of Psychiatry</u>, 1947). A patient believes that because two behaviors are paired, there is a cause and effect. For example, when a gambler wears a lucky hat, he thinks it causes him to pick a lucky number. When a patient prays to God to make him better, he attributes his recovery to the prayer.

At the Seventh Day Adventist Hospital in Celebration, prayer is considered part of the healing process.

Patients receiving prayer had "less congestive heart failure, required less diuretic and antibiotic therapy, had fewer episodes of pneumonia, had fewer cardiac arrests, and were less frequently intubated and ventilated" (Byrd, 1988, p. 829).

I have a male friend, 42, who in the last six months had 14 inches of his descending colon removed because of cancer. The surgeons probably also removed veins and arteries around the colon where cancer metastasizes. The work was done at the Mayo Clinic, Rochester, MN.

He came to Orlando to recuperate. Disney World, Universal Studios, the Holy Land Experience, Sea World and Aquatica, <u>et al</u>. + good weather, clean air and friendly people.

Further pain, x rays and upper GI endoscopy indicate polyps in his upper gastrointestinal tract. The surgeons removed them with a surgical snare. Later they cauterized them.

Now he is back for further surgical work.

I examined the 12 metal staples down the center of his chest, plus quarter inch tube that removes waste from his body. He also has the usual IVs for saline, pain killers and blood pressure monitoring.

RESEARCH

Medicine and science are great. They keep us alive and prolong the quality and quantity of our lives. But as I left the hospital room following our visit, I said, "Harry, don't be afraid to pray."

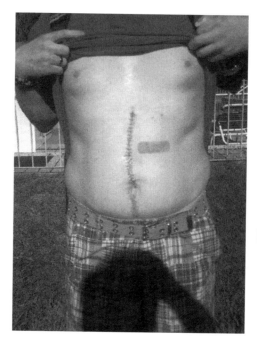

FADE OUT.

TITLE: BAD ACTORS (Rev #5) a screenplay posted on www.TriggerStreet.com.

Logline: a Femme Fatale, code named DOMINATRIX, tricks the modern descendants of Professor Moriarty and Sherlock Holmes to finance her Miami Models Agency.

MORIARTY, a paramilitary operative, gets his orders from VP DICK CHENEY. JACK HOLMES, the Director of the Secret Service, protects GOLD BULLION, on the Entertainment Train, Miami to NYC.

Dominatrix, an intel operative, tricks both men. Action, satire, eroticism, escapism. In the tradition of SOME LIKE IT HOT (1959).

FADE OUT.

Made in the USA
Middletown, DE
07 July 2016